LITTLE LIONS DONT LIE

A Lesson Learned:
Honesty is the best policy
A Kenny and Poochy Story

Robert Tripp

Copyright © 2021 by Robert Tripp

All rights reserved. No part of this publication may be reproduced, distributed, or transmitted in any form or by any means, including photocopying, recording, or other electronic or mechanical methods, without the prior written permission of the author who is the copyright owner, except in the case brief quotations embodied in critical reviews and other noncommercial uses permitted by copyright law.

ISBN: 978-1-63945-274-3 (Paperback)
        978-1-63945-275-0 (Hardback)
        978-1-63945-276-7 (E-book)

The views expressed in this book are solely those of the author and do not necessarily reflect the views of the publisher, and the publisher hereby disclaims any responsibility for them.

Writers' Branding
1800-608-6550
www.writersbranding.com
orders@writersbranding.com

Dedicated to
all children everywhere.

It was summertime, Kenny and his dog, Poochy, were having fun exploring the mountains and forest near their home.

Suddenly, Poochy said, "Look, Kenny, three lions are coming down the mountain.

It looks like a father lion, a mother lion, and a little lion. I'm scared. Should we hide?"

"No Poochy, they don't look mean, I will try to talk to them."

Kenny asked, "Lions, what are you doing here? We haven't seen lions like you on this mountain."

Father lion answered," We are on vacation and just passing through to a lion's convention."

"You are certainly welcome here," said Kenny, "We will introduce you to the other animals on the mountain."

"Thank you," replied father lion, "But, it looks like a storm, and we have to hurry on."

Just then it started to rain really hard.

"Hurry," said Kenny, "We have a special place out of the rain."

When Kenny, Poochy, and the lions came to Kenny's and Poochy's special place, other animals were also huddled there-an-eagle, a fox, a bear, and a coyote.

The eagle was the first to speak, he stretched forth his wide wings and proudly said,

"I am a mighty eagle, I will be the first to find the pot of gold!"

Eagles can fly high,
And look down from the sky;
My eagle eyes,
Will see the prize;
The pot of gold,
Will be mine to hold!

"Not so fast, eagle," said the fox.
"You are not so mighty, don't you know about foxes?"

Foxes are very smart,
They can't be caught;
Because I'm so clever,
The prize is mine forever;
The pot of gold,
Will be mine to hold!

Then the bear spoke, "Eagle and fox, do you really know about the mighty bear?"

Bears are big and strong,
Their search never goes wrong;
I know this mountain well,
The prize is mine to tell;
The pot of gold,
Will be mine to hold!

"None of you have a chance," said the coyote.
"Family and friends will help
me find the pot of gold!"

Coyotes are friendly, and fun,
As a family, we are one;
Working together is a treat,
The prize will be ours to keep;
The pot of gold,
Will be ours to hold,

Now, it was the lion's turn. Father lion said,
"To find the pot of gold would be nice,
but we must be moving on."

"But father," said little lion, "Lions are the mightiest of all.
You and mother can stay here with Kenny and Poochy,
I will find the pot of gold and make you proud."

Lions are the best, Far above the rest;
They don't know little lion son, The prize is already won;
The pot of gold, Will be mine to hold!

"Alright!" said father and mother lion together,
"But please be careful little lion."

"Open the sack little lion," shouted all of the animals,
"We want to see the pot of gold, we all tried hard
but we couldn't find it."

"No, I won't open the sack," said little lion,
"The pot of gold is mine, I found it. Father and mother
don't we have to be moving on?"

"Yes, we have to hurry," said father lion,
"But we all want to see the pot of gold."

Finally, little lion did open the sack.
What do you think was in the sack?
It wasn't a pot of gold - only old rocks!

Kenny, Poochy, and all of the animals shouted,
"Old rocks, not gold! Little lion has told a big lie!"

Little lion began to cry,
"Father, mother, I'm sorry, I only wanted to make you proud."

"You make us proud when you are honest," replied mother lion,
"Because you lied, we have lost precious trust."

Father lion added, "Also, the precious trust of Kenny and Poochy
and all of the other animals who have been so friendly and kind."

"Mother, father, Kenny and Poochy," said little lion,
"And, Eagle, Fox, Bear, and Coyote, I am really sorry."

Some Important Questions

1. Why did little lion tell such a big lie about finding the pot of gold?
2. It is said that everyone lies, some "big" lies and some little "white" lies. What are some of the reasons we tell lies?
3. When you lie, how does it make you feel?
4. When little lion lied, he lost some of the trust of his father and mother. How important is it to be trusted?
5. Why is "Honesty the Best Policy?"

www.ingramcontent.com/pod-product-compliance
Lightning Source LLC
LaVergne TN
LVHW071656060526
838200LV00030B/476